Undersea Volcanoes

Contents

Written by Inbali Iserles

Collins

The sizzling sea

Most people think of volcanoes as exploding peaks on tropical lands.

Fact

Volcanoes mainly form
under the sea.

Tectonic plates

Our planet is covered in a thin, hard crust.

the crust

rock and magma

liquid rock

hard rock

Like a giant jigsaw puzzle, the crust is made up of shifting slabs called tectonic plates.

5

Sometimes tectonic plates bump into each other, or pull apart.

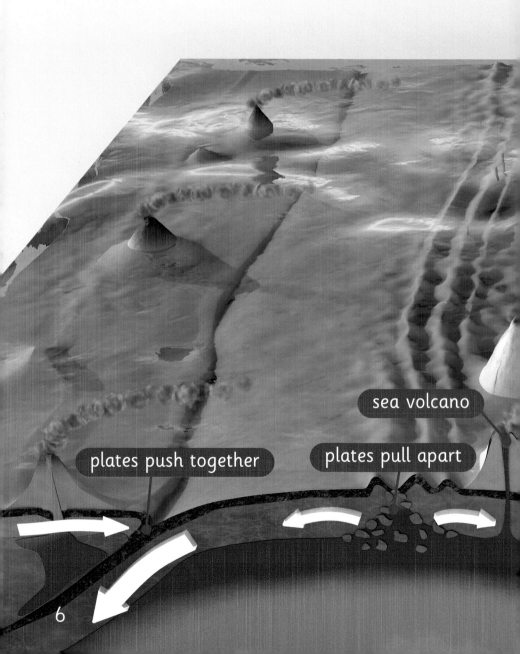

sea volcano

plates push together

plates pull apart

This can make mountains rise – and it can create volcanoes!

volcano on land

What is a volcano?

A volcano is an opening in the crust, often at the top of a hill or peak.

ash, steam and gas

main vent

cone

crust

magma

Bubbly gas and burning rocks
called magma rise up inside
the volcano from deep below
the ground.

Fact

When gas and magma get trapped,
they get pushed up inside
the volcano, making it **erupt**.

Some magma escapes volcanoes
as very hot liquid rock.

It is phenomenal when a giant volcano erupts.

The force can send out scorching magma, dusty wind and smelly gas for miles.

Volcanoes of the deep

Often, when an undersea volcano erupts, it cannot be felt from the beach.

Fact

There may be as many as 1,000,000 volcanoes below the sea!

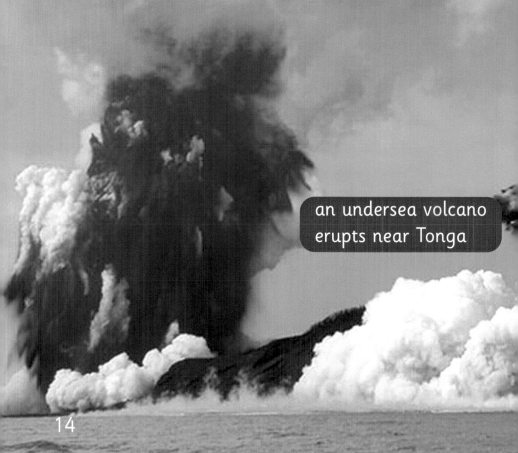

an undersea volcano erupts near Tonga

But when a massive volcano erupts, huge waves can cover the coast.

Sea vents

Undersea volcanoes are good news for sea life.
Gas rises from volcanic **vents** in fizzy streams.

The streams are full of tiny rocks called minerals. As the chilly sea cools the minerals, they harden into chimneys.

Tiny **microbes** feed on the minerals.

Amazing animals, like this crab, live near the chimneys. They feed on the microbes!

We still have a lot to discover about undersea volcanoes. Studying these habitats can help us to understand our planet. Was it in the deep, dark heat of the vents that life first began?

Glossary

erupt when a volcano ejects a lot of hot melted rock, as well as ash and gas

microbes tiny living things, which you can only see with a microscope

vents holes in the sea bed that let out magma or gas

Index

23

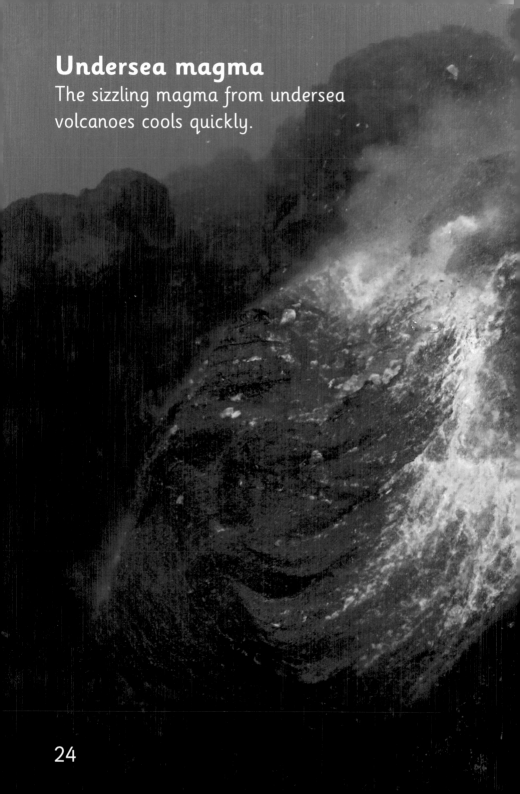

Undersea magma

The sizzling magma from undersea
volcanoes cools quickly.

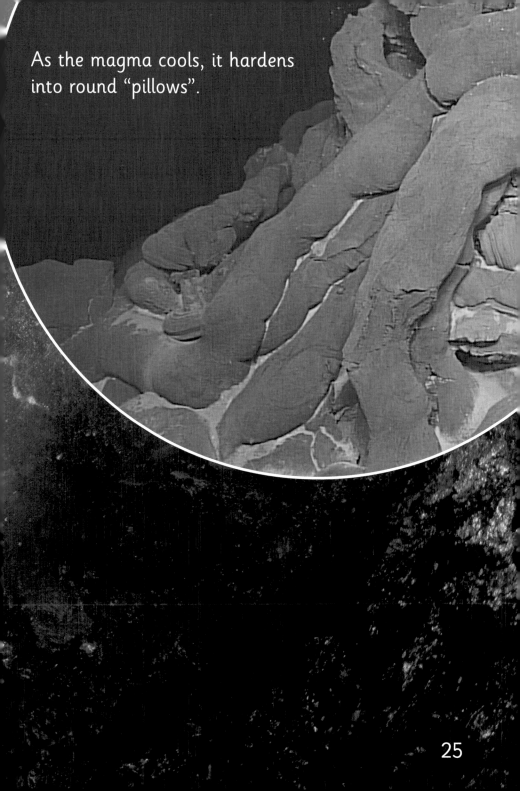

As the magma cools, it hardens
into round "pillows".

Spotted from above!

This volcano (spotted between Tonga and New Zealand) is probably the biggest undersea volcano. Someone on a plane spotted it by accident when she saw giant lumps of volcanic rock in the sea!

New Zealand

volcano

Iceland

The peaks of undersea volcanoes can slowly grow into new lands.

Iceland

Iceland was formed when undersea
volcanoes erupted.

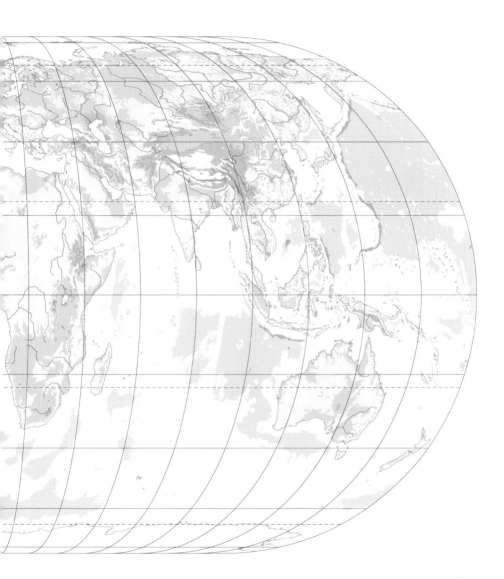

Undersea volcanoes

😺 Review: After reading 🐾

Use your assessment from hearing the children read to choose any GPCs, words or tricky words that need additional practice.

Read 1: Decoding

- Practise reading words that contain different spellings of the same sounds: /ee/, /l/ and /u/.

tiny	chimneys	minerals	puzzle	some	covered

- Ask the children to read pages 10 and 11 aloud. Say: Can you sound out and blend the words in your head as you read them aloud?
- Bonus content: Ask children to read page 26. Can they find the word in which the letter "c" makes two different sounds? (/c/ and /s/ in **accident**) Can they find another spelling of /s/ on page 29? ("c" in **Iceland**)

Read 2: Prosody

- Model reading pages 16-17, emphasising the key words in each sentence (e.g. **volcanoes** and **sea life** in the first sentence).
- Ask the children to read the pages, experimenting with emphasis to make the meaning clear.
- Point out the linking words. (*streams, minerals*)
- Ask the children to read the pages, experimenting with emphasis to make the meaning clear.

Read 3: Comprehension

- Ask the children whether they think volcanoes are exciting or dangerous, or both, and why?
- On page 4, point to the word **plates**. Ask: What are these **plates** made from? (*the earth's crust*) Why are they described as **slabs**? (*e.g. they are heavy, but thin and flat, like pavement **slabs***)
- Challenge the children to think of a synonym for each of these words, then try out their synonym in the sentence. Does it make sense? Discuss why some synonyms make sense, and why others do not.

  page 4: **crust**   page 16: **streams**   page 17: **chimneys**

- Turn to pages 30 and 31. Discuss how the pictures are connected. Ask: Do creatures benefit from how the earth's crust moves? (*yes, vents form, releasing minerals that sea life feeds on*)
- Bonus content: Discuss the word **pillows** on page 25. Ask: What other words or phrases would make sense? (*e.g. long lumps, soft-looking shapes*)